Christmas AT THE CABIN

Spin-off from Behind My Words

J.L. DRAKE

CHRISTMAS AT THE CABIN

SPIN-OFF OF BEHIND MY WORDS

Copyright 2020 © J.L. Drake

To the unforgettable Christmas of 1993. I can still hear the laughter.

CHAPTER 1

Spencer

I clicked on the music and let *Baby, It's Cold Outside* slide off the speakers while I poured a Christmas cocktail into a glass. Singing along to the music, I plucked a cherry from the dish and garnished the top of the festive drink.

I stepped into my pretty red shoes, courtesy of my Aunt Lisa, looked into the mirror, and smoothed my free hand down my very short nightdress.

Steam rushed across my face as I opened the door to the master bathroom, and the wet warmth of it coated my skin with promises to come.

Easing onto the velvet chair I had moved from my closet earlier this morning, I crossed my legs and shamelessly admired the view.

Water cascaded down the planes of his back, down

his rock-solid ass, and swirled around his feet. Slowly, I pressed the frosted glass to my lips and downed some of the cool, tasty drink. My legs pressed together, and my stomach coiled when my fiancé turned to lean back into the spray.

Like the snow outside, the soap made its way down, finding the paths and grooves of his body. It slid over his yummy stomach and dripped from his semi-hard erection.

"How can someone be this sexy?" I whispered to myself. The author in me started writing the scene, and I found myself getting incredibly turned on. I leaned forward and took another long sip. Finding the cherry with my tongue, I fiddled with it between the ice cubes. Sweet juice tantalized my taste buds and awakened my senses even further.

With all my focus on his stomach, my mesmerized gaze followed his hand as it moved across his hip to his erection where it tightened and gave him a few pumps.

I bit the cheery in two and swallowed it down in a gulp before I lazily dragged my eyes up his mountain of a body and reached his eyes that were now deeply focused on me.

A hungry expression flashed across his face as he kept a slow, steady pace on his erection. Loving that he was totally comfortable with our constant need to ravish each other, I leaned back and uncrossed my legs.

"Do it." His voice was husky and filled with lots of dirty promises. Blake was the definition of a detective—tall, dark, and quiet. The weight of what he saw every day shaped him into a perfect sexy, dark character in any book. Truth be told, he was the muse for the past three books I'd released this year.

"Spencer," he warned, and I snapped out of that fantasy and into this one.

I reached between my thighs and found myself wet and ready. Easing two fingers inside, I dropped my head back against the wall and matched his rhythm.

When I saw his neck twitch and knew he was enjoying the show, I lifted a leg and gently pressed down on the heel of my shoe, allowing it to settle into the velvet and giving him a lovely shot of my arousal.

"Mm," he growled loudly and stepped out of the spray, leaving the water running. Standing naked a foot away from me with water drops finding little spots to hide on his perfect body, he snatched my drink off the counter and downed the rest.

In a quick motion, he hooked his arms under my knees and pulled me down, so my back was flat. He dropped to his knees and shot me a wicked smile as he held an ice cube between his teeth. It protruded just a little. Before I could prepare, he swiped it in between my folds and sent a wild new sensation through my overheated body.

"God damn, Blake." I laughed and held his head in place as he licked, sucked, and dove around with ice cold lips. With one hand, he stroked the outside of my thigh and around my bare ass. He picked up the pace, and I could tell he was holding back when he really wanted to go crazy on me.

My heels and nails dug at his back, and my head whipped back and forth, so close to my own release.

"Blake, I'm so close."

He stood and hauled me down to the edge of the chair, holding my legs straight up, and plunged in deep. The base of his shaft smacked my opening, sending a delicious sound throughout the room. His thrusts nearly lifted me right off the chair.

"You're so damn gorgeous." He smiled down at me. "You fit me so damn well."

I smiled up at this beautiful man, the one I had fallen in love with while working on a case. A case that not only almost took my life, but sadly robbed me of the lives of my parents a year earlier. He was my hero, my protector, my real-life research partner. And boy, did I love our research moments.

His strong hands covered my bouncing breasts, and he kneaded them with a satisfied moan. His fingers pinched my nipples hard, and I shot off into a million colors as different degrees of heat licked my insides.

Blake always waited until I was completely satisfied before he would allow his own release. He bucked forward, nearly bending me in half, and buried his face in my chest.

"How can sex just keep getting better and better?"

"I have no idea." I laughed, feeling oh-so-good, but

then yelped when he pulled me up, still inside me, and walked us into the warm spray. Pressing my back into the shower wall, he kissed my neck and whispered all the things he loved about me.

Despite my past, hang-ups, near death experiences, and his, we had made it out to the other side better than ever.

"We're going to be late." He pulled me from my thoughts.

"What's one more round?" I kissed his jaw, wanting more.

"I promised your uncle we'd be there on time, and I have the truck, remember?"

"Remember?" I gave him a wicked smile. "How can I forget our snowstorm sex?" Last year, Blake and I were trapped on the side of the road, caught in one of the worst snowstorms New York had ever seen. Instead of being upset or cold, we found other ways to keep each other warm.

"We should really try that again sometime." He sucked my bottom lip into his mouth and laughed in his throat as he kissed me senseless.

Somehow, we untangled our bodies in time to get dressed and run out the door to the snow-covered beast that was his truck.

"Back inside, Lloyd." I shooed my brat-of-a-kitty back inside and blew my hound a kiss. Shutting the front door again, I heard a sound and walked around the other side of my patio to see my crazy neighbor, Shannan, knee deep in snow, pulling a tree across her lawn.

"Shannan?" I called and did my best to cover my laughter at the scene. My tiny bulldog of a neighbor, who was maybe four foot nine inches tall, give or take, was trying to move a tree about three times her size.

"Hey, babe," she huffed and fell backward, sending a puff of powered snow into the air like a bomb.

"Do you need help?"

"No," she popped up, "I'm making a point with Kim, that I can do this on my own."

I laughed lightly. She and her wife were like two little spitfires, always trying to be the one on top.

"Okay, well, good luck with that. We're heading to the tree lot, so be careful, okay?"

"Yes, go do it the easy way," she muttered, but I knew her mood was not directed at me.

I really wished I had a camera because it would make a pretty funny Christmas card.

I slipped into the truck and sighed happily.

"What was that all about?" Blake looked over at me, curious about what I witnessed.

"Shannan." I pulled my seatbelt across my chest and clicked it in place.

"Oh," he chuckled, "what is our sassy little neighbor up to today?"

"Seems she and Kim are in their annual argument on

what tree to get. Kim hates going out into the woods, and Shannan hates the tree lots. So now she's trying to give herself a hernia dragging a 'real' tree up across their property to prove her point that she can do it all."

"Have I ever mentioned how much I love that couple?"

"They truly are entertaining, aren't they?"

"Indeed." He reached for my hand and kissed the diamond he had given me just under a year ago. I wanted a summer wedding, and he wanted to wait until his brother Henry returned home from his year-long trip to Italy. I understood where he was coming from, but I wanted to be his, like, yesterday. I pushed that thought from my head and focused on the fact that we were together, here, healthy, and the rest could wait.

The roads weren't the best today, but it was only two days until Christmas, and we still didn't have a tree. We were, after all, hosting Christmas Eve dinner for my aunt and uncle—and, of course, our beloved crazy neighbors Kim and Shannan—so a tree, a big tree, was definitely needed.

"Looks like there's still some good ones left." Blake nodded at that and pulled into the tree lot where we quickly spotted my Uncle G, who also happened to be Blake's sergeant at the police department here in town.

"Hey." He pulled me into one of his famous bear hugs that always made me feel like I was six again. They were my favorite, and no matter what age I was, I would always treasure those hugs.

"Sorry we're late," I whispered over his shoulder.

"Don't be. Lisa is still at the market getting something for the pies." He rolled his eyes. My Aunt Lisa loved to be late for everything. "But she promised she'd join us as soon as she was finished." He turned his attention to my fiancé. "Blake." G shook his hand like they always did. I didn't know if it was because they worked so closely together or what, but the handshake seemed to serve as their version of a hug.

Rows and rows of trees stood tall and proud, each one hoping to be chosen to be in a window, beautifully decorated for all to see. A couple of young boys were constantly giving each one a shake to remove the softly falling snow from their branches so the customers could see their shape. I had to smile at their efforts. It was a losing battle, and I loved the way the snow looked on them, anyway.

"You're writing in your head again, aren't you?" Blake teased, and I smiled with a shrug.

"That obvious?"

"It's your face. You get this happy, content smile."

"Sorry. I can't turn it off even if I wanted to." The curse of a writer's head. It never stopped and always made us look at things just a little differently than the average person. I imagined it was something like Blakes's head, but I saw the beauty where he saw the flaws.

"Don't be sorry. It's kind of sexy."

"Oh, yeah?" I beamed up at him.

"Don't look at me like that." He leaned down and quickly kissed my lips. "After this morning, I can barely keep my hands off of you."

"What about this one?" G broke up our dirty play, and I hurried over to see what he had chosen.

"Seriously?"

"What?"

"This makes Charlie Brown's tree look positively bushy."

"Bushy?" He quirked an eye at my comment.

"I was hoping maybe we could pick one that would actually hold up an ornament. Not one that could possibly burst into flames the moment we put a light on it."

"Fine." He pronounced the word slowly. "What about that one?" He pointed to another sick- looking tree.

"That alley-cat looking tree?"

"Every year, Spence, every year we go around and around until you spot your perfect tree. And every year, I bet money that it will be one of the very first trees you saw when we came in."

"It's not my fault. I want the perfect tree."

"Good luck." G smacked Blake on the shoulder as I scowled at both of them.

I opened my mouth to make a scathing retort as my phone caught my attention. I held it up and removed myself momentarily from our annual bickering. I really enjoyed all the fun and games over the tree selection with Uncle G. Of course, I knew he was right. I usually spotted the one I wanted almost right away, but where was the fun in that? I dragged the whole experience out because it was so much fun stressing out my uncle over it, especially because I knew he truly enjoyed it, too.

"Hey, Jaci." I giggled into the phone. "What's up?"

"First, I wanted to know why you didn't return my call last night."

"Sorry, but Blake came home early, and, well, I came shortly after that." I laughed so hard I hiccupped into the phone.

"Nice," she drawled sarcastically. "Also, I hate your love life."

"Mm, I know."

"Whatever, I'll just live vicariously through your books."

"Atta girl." I shot Blake a dirty smile.

"Second, I'm officially inviting myself to Christmas Eve dinner."

"Great." I rolled my eyes. My best friend was a trip.

"I switched my shifts. Now I'm working New Year's but have both Christmas Eve and Day off. The *boyfriend* was supposed to do the same, but somehow, he managed to be working the opposite shifts, and I will not be left alone like a sad, pathetic loser, so I'm coming to party with you."

"Well, when you say it like that, sure." My phone buzzed, and I saw it was Aunt Lisa calling. "Jaci, can you hold on for a moment?"

"Yup."

"Hey, Lisa. Will you be joining us soon?"

"What, to watch you and G argue over a tree? Oh, I'm missing so much." She laughed, dripping in sarcasm.

"First, it's tradition, and second, where's the fun in missing G tossing his arms up when I point to the first tree we looked at?"

"Tape it for me?" She laughed again, and I moved around to see another rack of trees in the back corner of the lot. "I'm stuck in a line at the market because apparently everyone and their mother needs milk two days before Christmas."

"Got to love the holiday rush." My words trickled away when I spied Kim in the parking lot.

"Look, honey, I have to go, but I'll try to make the tree lot as soon as I can. If not, I'll see you later."

"Okay." I hung up, and two seconds later, the phone rang again.

"Seriously?" Jaci hissed, "You hung up on me?"

"Sorry." I felt like I was about to miss something good. "It was Lisa, and she was just checking in."

"Spence?" G held up his hand as I approached as if asking which tree I wanted. I pointed to the one I had seen at the start of our search and watched his face pink up. "See? Every year!"

I chuckled and went back to my call. "Okay, girlfriend, be at my place at five. Bring whatever or don't. Just remember, if you skip out on your cheesecake, the invite will be revoked next year."

"I'm making my list of ingredients now."

"And that's why I love you." She was a wonderful cook, and I took a moment to savor the idea of biting into her delicious cheesecake.

"Love you, too. Thanks, girl. I'll see you soon."

"I don't know why Shannan doesn't get it." Kim threw her arms in the air as she approached us. She entered the tree lot at full speed, her little legs working a mile a minute to gain ground on us. "Look at all these options, big, tall, skinny, fat, but no, my wife insists on heading into the wilderness like a lumberjack to go get a shrub." Her voice dripped with heavy sarcasm.

"Did you, by any chance, see her earlier?" I ventured, trying to keep my voice even.

"No, I refused to allow her to draw me into any part of trudging about the snowy woods in the freezing cold to hunt for a tree. I left after coffee." She fudged her frustration, but I knew they loved the banter just like the rest of us did. "So, I'm here to get a backup."

"Ah, yes." I smirked at Blake, who was listening from a safe distance.

"This one will do. See how easy that was?" She turned to the kid wearing work gloves. "This one."

"Do you have a truck you'd like me to put it in?"

"Nope." She nodded to her Volkswagen. "We're gonna strap it on that little baby, and I'm going to drive it home."

"Ah?"

"What, you scared of a challenge?"

"No, ma'am. But I'm nervous you won't be able to see out of the front windshield."

"I can barely see over the steering wheel as it is, young pup. I'll manage." Kim winked at me and hurried the boy along.

Blake had to turn around to hide his smile when G marched the tree I had chosen over to the checkout, grumbling the whole way. We both smiled as we watched him hand the guy the money and wait to have the trunk trimmed and the tree netted up tight.

"Such a great time of year." He wrapped his arm around me, and we joined G, who huffed at me but slapped a smile on when the fellow handed him the change.

CHAPTER 2

Shannan

"Oh, the weather outside sure sucks, but the fire is so delightful, and since my wife is so stubborn, let it snow, let me sweat, let me drink!" I sang and jammed the last metal pin into its trunk then waited a beat to see if it would stand up on its own.

"Yes!" I heaved and used my arm to dry my forehead. I sniffed when something strange passed by my nose. Odd.

I pulled out the photo once again and studied it for a moment. I held it up in front of the tree to see how all the white origami birds were situated on the branches.

Kim's mother would decorate their tree differently every year. Ever since I met Kim, she had always said her favorite tree was the one from when she was eleven and her mother spent hours folding little white origami birds.

She had dusted each one with silver glitter so they would catch the sparkle of the white twinkle lights. Her mother passed away a month ago, and I wanted to do something special for her.

"What the hell is that?" I sniffed again put couldn't place it.

I checked the time, knowing Kim would be home from the store soon, and my hike out of the woods had taken way too long.

Rushing to the spare room, I climbed the ladder to reach the shelf and pulled down the hidden shoe box. I was very proud of myself that I had started this project early. I had thirty-four birds ready to go with little clips glued to the bottoms to easily hook onto the branches.

I held up the string of lights and started to put them on the tree. The fine branches made it hard to keep them there, and I was glad no one was around to see how much I struggled to get them on.

Sure, they weren't on very evenly, and there were parts that were in clusters, but that was the first time I'd ever done the light bit, and I was pretty impressed.

One by one, I attached the birds, just like the photo, and even made sure they were all facing the correct direction. I was tempted to add a stuffed cat on the top with a mouth full of feathers, but I wasn't sure if she'd see the humor in that, given this was a sentimental tree.

"Just a few more tweaks, and there we go." I stepped

back and admired my work. It wasn't prefect, but hell, I'd bet Alfred Hitchcock would be proud. I thought it was perfect, and Kim was well worth the fuss.

"Okay, that's finished." I continued chatting to myself out loud, as it always brought me comfort, even as a child. "Oh, yes, the fire needs another log." I carefully placed a log and moved to the kitchen to see if her beers were chilled. "Yes. Everything is coming together." I held up my hands and saw the tips of a couple of my fingers were still white. Damn Raynaud's. It always kicked in when my hands got cold, and the tree branches were only just beginning to thaw. I glanced at the still empty driveway and quickly placed the bakery cookies on a plate and felt like everything was as good as it could be. I reached to turn off the TV, just catching the weather guy gloating about the fact that we were getting more snow tonight. Of course, we were.

I struggled into my favorite oversized sweater, which was really just a size medium, but when you were as short as I was—well, I liked to pretend it was size huge. Stepping out on the chilly patio, I waited to hear her car.

Twenty minutes later, I raced to the steps and was disappointed to see her face was far from festive.

"Hey," I stopped her from entering the door, "are you still mad over our tiff?"

"No." She sighed and brushed some pine needles off her coat. "Let's just say the corner of Carol Street and Radley has a tree now."

I glared at her. "I told you I had it covered."

"Mm…" She waited for me to move, but when I didn't, she crossed her arms, unamused. "What?"

"I did something."

"Oh, sweet Jesus, what now?"

"First, thank you." I swatted her arm. "Second, I did some digging and got a bit creative, and well…" I stepped back and let her pass and waited to hear her excitement.

"Why does it smell like cat piss in here?"

"What?"

She started to cough, and her eyes went red. "Was Lloyd here? Did he spray?"

"No. What are you talking about?" I raced in and turned the corner and took a huge whiff. "Oh, my God." I wanted to barf. "Where is that coming from?"

"Oh, wow, babe," she whispered through a cough, "that's just like the one my mother made!"

"This was supposed to be special. Not smell like a week-old litter box. I don't understand."

Kim moved over and rubbed the tree branch between her fingers. "You picked a cat-piss spruce, not a Douglas fir."

"Huh?" I was so confused. A Christmas tree was a Christmas tree.

"This is a white spruce, commonly known as a cat-piss spruce." Her smirk slipped out, and I wanted to scream, only the idea of letting that smell inside my body again made me internalize my rage.

"This is one of the most thoughtful things you've ever done, babe, but it needs to go!"

With defeat and disappointment heavy on my chest, I started to remove the birds as Kim answered her phone.

"Hey, Blake." She looked at me strangely. "Yeah, Shannan still is. Of course, um, yeah, I can meet you." She paused. "Okay, I can come now."

Seriously?

"Blake needs my help. I'll explain everything later. Wait for me to come home, and I'll help take this out. For now, just open some windows."

"Bleach wouldn't even help this smell, Kim."

"Hey," she held my face so I could see her soft expression, "no one has ever done anything as thoughtful as that for me before. I'm incredibly touched, and once we get a new tree up, I can't wait to admire it. Please don't take me leaving as anything but wanting to help out a friend. I assure you, it's not because every time I swallow, I'm tasting cat urine." She smothered her hearty laugh with a hand.

"Jerk." I laughed with her and shook off some of my disappointment. I had so wanted it to be absolutely perfect. She gave me a quick kiss and left.

When it came to Spencer or Blake, we'd drop anything we were doing to help them out. After Spencer's parents died, we watched her like a hawk, and it was only in the past year we'd seen her turn a new leaf and be happy. She was like our adopted child, not that we'd ever say that out loud when her aunt was around. Lisa couldn't have kids and had latched on to that little girl the moment she met her years ago. I chuckled at the thought of how we were all so protective of that young woman, and now add her sexy detective fiancé to the mix, and it was an interesting cocktail.

"Okay, time to go." I started the process all over again but in reverse.

Forty-five minutes later, I had the tomcat out the door and onto the deck, where I risked my life to bend it over the railing to let it tumble to the ground.

"You get to stay there," I hissed and pulled out my phone to Google the correct kind of tree.

As much as I wanted to race off to the tree lot and do this the easy way, I would not. I needed to keep some of my pride. Besides, my freakin' luck, I'd run into Kim, and all my talk about my family memories of hunting for the perfect tree, smelling the fresh snow, listening to it crunch under my boots, and starting snowball fights would be lost in one moment.

No, I could do this.

I was sure I looked like Maggie from *The Simpsons* in my wet snowsuit. It was so tight it forced my short t-rex arms out straight, and the stiff fabric from the pants made me walk like I couldn't bend my knees. Being short sucked.

With an axe over my shoulder, I headed back into the woods, determined to find the perfect tree for my wife.

CHAPTER 3

Spencer

The stunning ten-foot tree stood proudly in the bay window, casting its colors out onto the fresh snowdrifts on the deck. Ornaments from my childhood hung from the branches with their memories of simpler, happier times. I reached out to touch my favorite, an ages-old Santa, minus his arms, but it still had its red twist-tie legs and little pink face. It was the ugliest thing, but it had belonged to my dad, and I wouldn't dream of not hanging it on the tree. I had placed our old silk tree skirt around the bottom to cover the stand and chuckled at the missing bits of white fur that outlined its edges. Lloyd had attacked and removed chunks of it before I could catch him. I knew I had to keep an eye on that little devil. I planned to pay him back by making him wear a sparkly Christmas collar.

Garland draped the length of the mantel, and woven amongst it were sparkly leaves from a bright red poinsettia that caught the flicker from the candles.

A sleigh lay next to the comforting fire and held a supply of birch wood just waiting to warm the chilly hands of those about to arrive.

My favorite Christmas carol, *Have Yourself A Very Merry Christmas*, was playing softy from the speakers, and I grinned, thinking how proud my parents would be if they could see me now.

I whirled around and spotted my phone on the table. I tapped on Blake's name and reached for my hot chocolate and Bailey's.

"Hey, hun." He sounded a bit off.

"Hey, I, ah, was wondering if you wanted me to meet you in town, and we could grab something to eat. I've been decorating all afternoon and have zero desire to cook."

"Sorry." He covered the mic of the phone with something, as it sounded muffled. "I'm running around at the moment and think I might be a bit later tonight than expected."

A ping of disappointment raced through me. Blake had been working crazy hours lately. I hated that I wanted to spend so much time with him. I wasn't the needy type; I just wanted him near.

"Okay, I'll figure something out."

"Oh, wait. Kim wants to ask you a question."

"Okay." *Wait, what?*

"Hey, lovely, we have a lasagna in the fridge that you are more than happy to have, but listen, Shannan tried to do something really special for me today, and it backfired. I was hoping you could go see if she needs some company?"

"Ah, sure."

"Thanks, love. Just make sure you hold your nose."

"What?" I chuckled in confusion.

"I have to go, Spence." Blake was on the phone again. "I'll call you on my way home. Love you."

"Sure thing. Love you, too." I saw the line had disconnected, and I slipped off the stool. I was pleased that Kim and Blake were hitting it off. They had a lot in common and loved to banter with one another. I was so happy Blake loved my friends just as much as I did.

The air was freezing, and the snow still fell steadily, but at least the wind wasn't overly strong when I stepped outside and headed along the beaten path between my place and Kim and Shannan's. A couple of weeks ago, Blake had strung some colored lights through the trees to help guide us as we walked between the two homes. I took a moment to stop and listen to the silence the winter brought. Breathing in deeply, I let the cold fill my lungs then released it in a huff of white cloud that drifted away without a care in the world. I loved winter.

My stomach growled and begged me to move on. Once I got to the clearing and approached the house, I rushed up the back deck steps and spotted a tree stuck upside down in the snow.

What on Earth happened here?

Using the side of my palm, I brushed away the frost on the sliding glass door and peered inside. The fire was dying, and there was a cluster of lights and paper birds flung on the couch.

"Shannan?" I knocked on the door and waited to see if she was there.

Nothing.

"Shannan," I tried again and played dirty, "Blake asked if you could help him out. He's in the hot tub."

Nothing.

Normally, when it came to anything to do with Blake, she'd come running out of a room so fast she'd hit the wall like a puppy excited for a treat.

Okay, so, she's not here.

I spotted the terrifying gnome Shannan got Kim a few years ago and pulled back its velvet hat to reveal the patio door key. I quivered inside at its happy, psychotic expression and decided to turn it slightly so it couldn't watch me.

"Shannan, if you're here, it's just me, Spencer, coming to steal some lasagna." All was quiet, but as I moved farther into the house, there was a smell of something awful. I peeked out the window to see that her car was not in the driveway.

"Oh, please, don't be the food." My tummy took

over my thoughts. I pulled out the dish and was relieved to know it wasn't the lasagna that smelled and popped it on a paper plate, pleased that I didn't have to stay here to eat it. I wrapped it in tin foil, and once it was ready to go, I scribbled a note for Shannan to find when she got home.

Hey, Kim asked me to come by and check on you. Text me when you get home. Yes, it was me who took the corner piece of the lasagna. Yum! Spencer xo - P.S. Your place smells like you just killed someone. Pro Tip: Maybe a little less ammonia next time.

I drew a heart and hurried outside to take a deep breath of fresh air. With a quick scan of their dock and tree line, I concluded she must have gone into town.

"Meow." Llyod screamed his needy cry from a rock by the path.

"What?"

"Meow!" He pawed at the snow then held up a paw like the snow was too cold for His Highness. I rolled my eyes, knowing what he wanted.

"I swear you're near sixty pounds. The twenty feet to the front step will do you some good." I waved at him to follow me. "Come on." He just glared at me, knowing I'd give in. "Fine." I walked back and awkwardly scooped the little crap off the ground and carried him back to the house. I dumped him on the entry way mat as I kicked off my snow boots. He hissed as if to give me the finger, and with his tail straight up in the air, he swaggered over and snuggled in with the dog in front of the fire.

"You're welcome." I snickered as I went to warm up my dinner.

With a full tummy, a glass of wine, and a hot date with Tom Hardy, I made it roughly twenty minutes into the movie before I gave in to sleep.

Something warm touched my face, and I moved into it, wanting more.

"Hey, baby." Blake's voice made me smile as I pulled myself from the dark bliss. Blinking a few times, I found him sitting on the coffee table across from me.

It took me a moment to realize it was still nighttime out. "Did you just get in?"

"Yeah, about ten minutes ago." He leaned down and gave me a soft kiss. "Did you get something to eat? I brought you some Chinese in case you didn't."

I loved that he thought to do that. "I did, but I will gladly have that tomorrow."

"Okay, I'm going to go change, and I'll meet you back here in—" He stopped when he tuned in to someone walking up the steps.

"Who's that?"

"Not sure." He headed over to the door. I noticed his posture became tense when he checked the window and opened the door.

"Hey, is Shannan here?"

I pushed the blanket off and met Kim as Blake stepped back to welcome her inside.

"No." I crossed my arms at the sudden rush of cold that followed her in. "I went over earlier, and she wasn't there, but her car was gone, so I figured she was in town."

"Her car is at Jeff's getting the brakes repaired." I could tell she was worried, so I instantly went to her and gave her a reassuring hug.

"Blake, can you call her?" Kim asked and shot me a look. She didn't need to explain. We all knew Shannan's love for him.

"Straight to voicemail." His tone told me he was kicking into work mode. "When was the last time you spoke with her?"

"I was with her when you called earlier, and that was it." Suddenly, something hit her. "Oh, shit."

"What?" he asked.

"She's so damn stubborn!"

"Kim, what?" I touched her arm, growing more concerned by the second.

"I can bet you any money she went out looking for another tree."

"Is that why there's a tree upside down in the yard?"

"Yeah," she shook her head, "she was trying to re-enact a childhood memory for me, and it backfired because she chopped down a white spruce, and it made the whole house smell like cat piss."

"Oh!" Everything clicked for me. "That's what the smell was. Yeah, not a good tree at all."

"I never thought she'd go back out to get another." Kim rubbed her eyes as Blake handed me a flashlight. I immediately tugged on my boots and jacket.

"Let's go see if we can find her. It'll be hard because the snow would have covered her tracks by now, but hopefully, she didn't get too far."

We headed across the property and disappeared into the woods, each taking turns calling her name into the frigid night air.

A few times, I slipped, but Blake was right there to help me. "Please be careful, hun, I need you walking."

I chuckled at his comment and tried to be mindful of where I stepped.

"Shannan!" Kim was ahead of us. Her flashlight scanned back and forth near the base of the tree trunks, while she struggled forward through the snowdrifts. Though the thick branches provided a degree of protection from the snowfall, some places were much deeper than others.

By minute fifty-six, Kim's tone had changed from nervous to full-out panic mode. Not that I was ready to admit it yet, but I was starting to worry, too.

Blake was calculating time, versus steps, versus where the cluster of Douglas fir were. I found his detective head fascinating.

Kim grabbed my arm and stopped me mid-step. It was hard to see her face, but I could tell by the way she was breathing, bad thoughts had worked their way into her head.

"Hey," I covered her glove with my mitten, "we made a deal no one else was allowed to leave." I squeezed her hand, referring to the loss of my parents. "We all agreed. Right?"

"Right." She took an uneasy breath. "Right, that's right."

We continued to call as we trudged through the deepening snow, each of us deep in our own thoughts, trying to keep our worry from each other. The night was so cold, and the darkness suddenly seemed ominous when you considered someone dear to us could be lost and freezing and possibly frightened out there.

Blake suddenly rushed ahead. "Shannan!" he called, and I followed the beam from his flashlight to see what looked like a strange ghostly shape struggling to walk toward us.

"Shannan?" Kim raced toward her.

"The neighbors are going to call the police if you all keep on yelling my name." Her voice came from under the bushy tree she struggled with. "Step away from this tree." Her exhausted tone held a spark of defiance as Kim tried to hug her. "I'm not leaving here without it. It's damn well going up in our living room if it kills me."

"Fine, but put the damn thing down for a minute." Kim pulled her into her arms for a hug then checked her over. "Are you crazy going out alone like this? Are you freaking kidding me? Do you even know where you are?" she sputtered. "You're freezing, and you are damn lucky we found you. What the hell were you thinking?"

"What on Earth?" I came up behind Kim.

"A tree! It's almost midnight, and you're carrying a tree out of the woods!"

Shannan shrugged even as she shivered. "I told you I wanted to get the perfect tree, one that doesn't smell like piss, so here I am, getting it."

"You're crazy. You are a damn crazy, beautiful woman." Kim finally let her worry go and hugged her again. "Seriously, you scared me half to death."

"Us. You scared us half to death," I joined in.

"I'm sorry." She directed her apology to Blake, who leaned down and hugged her hard. "Oh, well, maybe it was worth it in more ways than I thought. How about a little tongue, darlin'?" She managed a laugh as Blake chuckled and swatted her arm playfully.

"I was five minutes away from calling it in to the station."

"Oh, please, no need for that."

"At least let me help you with the tree." Blake took the tree from Shannan, and we started the long walk back home. I was happy he knew the way, because I was completely turned around.

"Babe," Kim said when we finally arrived back to the

edge of the property.

"Yeah?"

"Promise me one thing?"

"Maybe." She chuckled, but when she looked over at her wife's expression, she knew it was a bit too soon to joke. "Okay, sure."

"Next year, we do the tree lot."

Shannan leaned her head on her shoulder. "Fine. But remember a girl can change her mind."

"Let's get you into a warm bath, pour a drink, and put this sucker up. Then, after that," she wiggled her eyebrows, "we can have a little Christmas fun with that whipped eggnog." She ogled her wife as we all laughed.

We said our goodbyes and headed along the path back to the cabin. Once inside, we both took a moment, beyond relieved that everything had turned out all right. We all had been through enough the past few years, and it was definitely time for things to get better.

I barely made it through the door before Blake turned me around, pressed me into the door, and kissed me hard.

"The whole time," his lips brushed over mine, "I was thinking what if that was you lost in the woods."

I ran a finger down his stressed face and realized how serious he was.

"I'm not sure what I would have done."

"You would have done exactly what you did to find Shannan, and you would have found me because you are damn good at your job, Blake. I admire how talented you are with that sexy head of yours."

He pressed his forehead to mine with a sigh.

"Come on. Let's go to bed."

He nodded and followed closely as we turned off the lights, locked up, and headed to the bedroom.

We lay in bed, Blake wrapped around me from behind, watching the snow fall outside our window. It sparkled as it passed through the beam of light from the outside lamp.

I closed my eyes, living in the moment, happy in the knowledge that at this point in time everyone I loved was safe and sound.

CHAPTER 4

"Blake?" I called from the top of the steps. "Are you ready?" He had been up since five working on something for G. I didn't want to point out it was Christmas Eve day. I knew he needed to busy himself with work. Last night seemed to shake him slightly.

"Yeah, I'm ready."

I threaded my mother's diamond earrings on and hurried down the stairs to grab my phone and purse.

"You look good." Blake's gaze dragged up my body, and I could almost feel the heat from it.

"Thanks." I glanced in the mirror at my tight jeans, knee high boots, white sweater, and bracelets stacked up on one wrist.

Blake came up behind me, his eyes dancing in excitement.

"Don't even," I warned but couldn't help but lean back into him when he pressed me to his front.

"I'll behave for now." He winked. "Let's get going."

Blake had already used the snowblower on our driveway, and apparently on Kim and Shannan's, who had already left for G's holiday brunch. Someone was eager this morning.

Fifteen minutes later, we were standing outside G's bright red door with a plate of homemade Nanaimo bars, his favorite.

Blake opened the door and let me walk in first, always such a gentleman. I got two feet in the door before I came to halt, completely taken back by the decorations that were in front of me.

"Holy…" I whispered at the dozens of sparkly snowflakes that hung from the ceiling, the endless yards of garland that outlined every doorframe and window, and the pissed off cat in the corner dressed in a little Santa suit. I made a mental note to get one of those for Lloyd the next time the little bugger ticked me off.

"Merry Christmas." Lisa popped out of nowhere, looking amazing in a holiday dress and her signature red heels.

"Merry Christmas." I laughed as Blake zipped by me while I handed Lisa the treats. "Did you do all of this? It's positively amazing."

"I did a little." She winked and directed me to the kitchen. "May I get you something to drink?"

"Sure." I looked around and spotted everyone in the living room. Lisa poured me an orange juice with a splash of grenadine. "Thanks."

"I wanted to give you this now." She reached back to grab a thin box.

"Oh, Lisa, thank you. You didn't need to do that."

"Please." She waved a hand for me to open it. Nestled inside the silver tissue paper was a silver chain with two hearts linked together. Engraved on the edge were the words *mother* and *daughter*. "It looked too cluttered to put 'stepmother' or 'second mother,' but I just want you to know we will always be connected and that I love you as if you were my own daughter."

"Oh, Lisa." I came around the counter and hugged my aunt. She had always tried so hard to be the mother figure in my life since my own mother had been taken from me. "It's beautiful. Thank you!"

"So," she turned me around to fasten the chain, "I heard your night was pretty eventful."

"A little, yeah." I laughed, admiring the pendant. "I'm just so glad she's all right. Kim was close to a heart attack."

"Poor thing." She looked over my shoulder then lit right up. "Well, then, let's make sure this is a Christmas to remember."

"Cheers to that." I took a sip of my drink and followed her into the living room where everyone was sitting around facing the TV. Kim had Shannan's hand, G waited for Lisa to join him, then he tucked her under his arm. And *Jaci?* I had no idea she was coming to this. She beamed at me and swooped me into a hug.

"Merry Christmas Eve!" I hugged her back tightly, so happy she was there. She then nodded at Henry, Blake's brother, who apparently had come home for Christmas, and their parents were here too. Wow!

I hurried over and gave Henry a hug. "What are you doing here?"

"I couldn't miss Christmas." He grinned and moved to let me greet his parents. Henry turned me around to see Blake coming toward me.

"Can I give you my present now?"

"Ah," I stumbled, confused on why he wasn't waiting until tomorrow. "Sure."

"Good. Here, sit." He pointed to the chair, and I sat, glancing at Jaci, who just shrugged.

"I know I have been a bit busy lately, but I wanted this to be special. First, I want to give a big shout out to Kim and to Lisa and G for all their help on this. Okay," he pushed a button on the TV, "here we go."

My parents popped up on the screen as they danced at their wedding. My hands flew to my mouth at the sudden flood of emotion that rushed through me. My mother's stunning white dress floated around my father as they waltzed to an old classic. The video switched to them racing down the steps of G's house and out onto the snowy lawn to take photos and celebrate. Slowly, it faded to my brother being carried through the door after he was born and to their old dog who was obviously unsure who the new intruder was. Again, it faded then went to my mother in her rocking chair that now sat at the cabin, and to me as a newborn lying on her chest as she sang me a song. Tears streamed down my face as I watched the screen. Most of the footage I had never seen before.

"Spencer." My father's voice could be heard as he called from another room, and I went running out in my Little Red Riding Hood dress to see my dad wearing a Big Bad Wolf outfit.

"Daddy!" I screamed and leaped into his arms, clearly excited he was joining in on the fun.

I dried my cheeks as I laughed along with the rest of the room.

The next was of us swimming at the lake after my parents bought the land our cabin now sat on. It wasn't long before the videos became just the three of us. My brother had turned to drugs by that time and was rarely at home. But, to my surprise, it didn't bother me, because I was seeing my parents happy, and that was all that mattered right now.

"Wow." Jaci laughed as G popped up on screen with a full-on light blue velour outfit.

"God, look at those thighs." He whistled at himself.

Next was a video of me behind my desk at the cabin, working away on my books with earphones in. My dad was behind the camera.

"Who would have thought my baby would be a best-selling author?" His voice was so proud. "She's something else, isn't she?"

"She sure is," Lisa agreed, and I looked over and gave her a smile. She mouthed, "So proud."

I blew her a kiss and went back to watching. After a few more memories rolled past, and I felt like I was ready to sob with happiness, the movement on the screen went still on a picture of a snowy window and scrolling appeared.

Philip and Molly Peters — Married 12/24/1974

Blake and Spencer Daniels — Married 12/24/2020

My gaze jolted to Blake and then to Shannan, who stood and pulled out a small book.

"I know how much you miss them, and I know this isn't bringing them back, but maybe we can marry on the same day they did." Blake's voice filled the room.

I swallowed hard, unsure if I could stand. So many emotions were already at the surface, but this one, this feeling that flooded my whole body, was one I had never felt before. Pure, unbelievable happiness.

Blake pulled me to my feet and took both my hands in his.

"You always said you wanted a small, intimate wedding, just the ones you love, no dress, no fuss. Well, here we are, with your parents in our hearts, standing in the same room where they were joined together." He paused while I let out a small sob, and he gently wiped the tears from my cheeks. "Spencer Peters, will you marry me right here, right now, so you can be mine forever?"

"Yes, yes," I cried as everyone stood and clapped. Whoops of joy filled the room while G pushed forward a small raised platform for Shannan to stand on.

As she spoke her sweet words, and my family stood all around us, for just a frozen moment in time I could feel my parents in the room as if they had never left. Although the pain of them being gone would never leave, tiny cracks in my heart started to heal.

Blake slipped a ring on my finger, and I did the same as his lips sealed with mine. We only pulled apart at the sound of a cork being pulled on a bottle of champagne.

"Sorry. Guess that was premature," Kim apologized.

The entire room broke into laughter as we finished the ceremony.

Pictures were taken, kisses were given, and we partied well into the holiday night.

***

"Mrs. Daniels," Blake called from downstairs.

"Yes, Mr. Daniels." I grinned into the mirror.

"Our guests are on their way over, and the turkey is about fifteen minutes from being finished."

"Okay!" I rushed downstairs just in time as I heard their footsteps stomping outside the door.

"I have cookies, I have stuffing, and most importantly, I have gin!" Kim announced as she and Shannan burst through the door looking dressed to kill in their ugly Christmas sweaters.

"You had me at gin." I laughed and took the plate of treats from her hand and nodded for Shannan to leave the stuffing on the counter.

"Merry Christmas, married lady." Kim kissed my cheek as Shannan gave me a hug, then they both headed over to the fireplace, still holding hands. Kim wouldn't let her out of her sight, poor thing. "Damn, these Dachshund legs are not meant for that much snow."

"It has been a lot so far this year, hasn't it?"

"Yes, I thought global warming was on my side, but apparently it's a man, so, you know." Kim struggled. "He's indecisive."

"Speaking of men…" Shannan peeked down the hallway.

"He went to get some more wood."

"Is he chopping it too?" She gave me a dirty wink.

"Possibly." I handed them a drink, and they gladly took it.

"Cheers to a year of loss, pain, and gain." Kim clicked

my glass and did the same to Shannan. As she took a sip, she coughed, trying to catch her breath at how strong I made it. "You," *cough-cough*, "always were my favorite."

"Just followed my father's recipe."

"Oh, yes," she laughed with tears, "what did he call it?"

"Just the drink to get through the Donalds' holiday party." We said it together, and we all laughed at how true it was. The neighbors on the other side of us had the most boring Christmas parties. No alcohol, homemade music, and sugar-free treats. It was the worst, but we did it with a little help from Dad's drinks.

"You better not have started without me." Jaci struggled to hold her bags and cheesecake when a hand appeared out of nowhere and helped her before it all fell.

"Thanks, G," she said over her shoulder, and I waited like a kid in a candy shop for my uncle and aunt to see how I had decorated the cabin.

"Wow." G beamed as he stepped inside and choked back some emotion. "Spence…you…it's just like—"

"Is it right?"

"Yes, it's as if time has gone backward." He wrapped me in his bear hug and reached for Lisa, who was in awe, too. "You did a wonderful job."

"Oh, honey, look at what you did," Lisa cooed. "It's perfection."

"Thank you." I wiped a tear, just knowing my parents

were back sitting in the room admiring the view. It had been far too long since the cabin had seen a Peters Christmas.

Bentley, my parents' hound dog, lifted his head to see who was here then dropped it back down with a heavy huff. Apparently, we were disturbing his nap. I didn't want to point out the fact that Lloyd the asshole cat had taken over his bed in front of the fire again. Maybe they had a truce and were finally co-existing because there was no other way around it. Either way, I was happy to see they were getting along.

"Ah," Jaci looked horrified, "those are some," she swallowed dramatically, "pretty sweaters you got there."

Kim, who loved making Jaci cringe at any point, sent me one of her intrigued smiles, and I knew the Christmas games had begun. "Thanks. I made it from real cat hair."

"Cat hair?" Each word jumped from her tongue like it stung her to even repeat it.

"Yes, it's been a six-month project." She leaned down and patted Lloyd to drive her sick point home.

"That's disgusting." She couldn't hold it back any longer, and Kim's delight was evident.

"Touch it." She used her pointer finger and rubbed the nasty wool around in a circle.

"This is why I don't leave the city." Jaci tossed her hands up and moved across the room toward me while Shannan, nearly in tears, high fived her.

"I'm concerned for you, Spencer." Jaci gave a pointed look toward Kim, who was still playing her part, and I chuckled, loving the lightness of the evening.

"Don't be." I spotted Blake as he returned from the shed with an armful of snowy wood and chuckled when Shannan made a beeline for him.

The table was set with red and gold coloring, and a little angel sat in the center. It spun slowly as the heat from the flame moved it around, sending a tinkling sound through the room. Lisa helped me bring the food to the table while Shannan opened the wine bottles.

"All right," I called everyone's attention, "dinner is ready."

Warmth spread through my body as I glanced at all those who sat around the table. Laughter and love shone from each and every one of them. My eyes sought Blake's and held his loving gaze as he lifted his glass to me with a look of pure lust that I would be sure to address later. To think if I had continued to live in my sad bubble and not let anyone else in, I would not have this. I drank deeply and returned his look with a promise.

The End

ACKNOWLEDGMENTS

To my mother, who is always right there willing to help, listen to me spin, laugh or cry. I love that we have this.

To my sister Erin, for always cheering me on and challenging me to write lighter.

To Alison Mello, who rose to the challenge right along with me to see if we could both write a Christmas story in a weekend. Mission accomplished!

To my beloved betas, Kim, Vanessa, Veronica, Elizabeth and Jamie for your eyes, support and advice.

To Spencer and Blake, for talking loud enough to me that I wanted to write you something special for the holidays.

And of course, to my readers, who allow me to toss dark or light stories at you without any warning!

SUGGESTED READING ORDER

World One
(All books connect in World One) Broken
Shattered
Mended
Honor
Escape
Trigger
Demons
Unleashed
Freedom
Omertà
Courage
Darkness Lurks
Darkness Follows
Darkness Falls

World Two
(Not connected to World One)
Behind My Words
Christmas at the Cabin
All In
Quiet Wealth

ABOUT THE AUTHOR

Author J.L. Drake was born and raised in Nova Scotia, Canada, later moving to Southern California where she lives with her husband and two children.

When she's not writing she loves to spend time with her family, traveling or just enjoying a night at home. One thing you might notice in her books is her love for the four seasons. Growing up on the east coast of Canada the change in the seasons is in her blood and is often mentioned in her writing.

Her books can be found in different languages around the world.

You can connect with J.L. Drake on Facebook, Instagram, Twitter, BookBub, and Goodreads!

You can also check out her website at www.authorjldrake.com.